"Liz," Jessica yelled from the bedroom window. "Do you want to watch *Sleeping Beauty* with me?"

Elizabeth shaded her eyes with one hand. "Not now, Jess. I'm still practicing."

"Wouldn't you like to watch this ballet movie instead? The dancers have beautiful costumes on," Jessica called.

"I have to keep practicing," Elizabeth called. She looked at the ground. "If I don't practice, I won't be good enough to make the team."

Jessica let out a loud sigh. It looked like ballet was one thing that she would have to do without her twin.

SWEET VALLEY KIDS

FEARLESS ELIZABETH

Written by
Molly Mia Stewart

Created by
FRANCINE PASCAL

Illustrated by
Ying-Hwa Hu

A BANTAM SKYLARK BOOK®
NEW YORK · TORONTO · LONDON · SYDNEY · AUCKLAND

RL 2, 005–008

FEARLESS ELIZABETH
A Bantam Skylark Book / February 1991

Sweet Valley High® and Sweet Valley Kids are
registered trademarks of Francine Pascal

Conceived by Francine Pascal

Produced by Daniel Weiss Associates, Inc.
33 West 17th Street
New York, NY 10011

Cover art by Susan Tang
Skylark Books is a registered trademark of Bantam Books, a division of
Bantam Doubleday Dell Publishing Group, Inc. Registered in U.S. Patent
and Trademark Office and elsewhere.

ISBN 0-553-15844-9

Published simultaneously in the United States and Canada

Bantam Books are published by Bantam Books, a division of Bantam Doubleday Dell Publishing Group, Inc. Its trademark, consisting of the words
"Bantam Books" and the portrayal of a rooster, is Registered in U.S. Patent
and Trademark Office and in other countries. Marca Registrada. Bantam
Books, 666 Fifth Avenue, New York, New York 10103.

PRINTED IN THE UNITED STATES OF AMERICA

OPM   0 9 8 7 6 5 4 3 2 1

To Kimberly Bloom

CHAPTER 1

Recess!

Elizabeth Wakefield held her breath while she watched the minute hand of the classroom clock. At last, it ticked to eleven-forty, and the bell rang for recess.

Everyone in Mrs. Otis's second-grade class closed their books and raced for the door.

"Do you want to play jump rope?" Jessica Wakefield asked.

Elizabeth looked at her twin sister and shook her head. Jumping rope was one of Jessica's favorite recess games, but it wasn't one of Elizabeth's.

Even though they were identical twins, Elizabeth and Jessica liked different things. Elizabeth enjoyed climbing trees and making up adventure stories like the ones she read in books. She loved school, too, and always got good grades.

Jessica didn't like school. Sometimes she passed notes and whispered to her friends during class. After school, she preferred indoor games that didn't mess up her clothes, like playing with dolls or pretending to be a movie star.

From the outside, Jessica and Elizabeth looked exactly alike. Both girls had blue-green eyes and long blond hair with bangs. When they dressed in the same outfits, their friends often couldn't tell them apart. The only way to be sure who was who was by checking their name bracelets.

Despite their differences, the twins were best friends. They shared a bedroom. They loved to pick out their clothes together every morning. And sometimes they even finished each other's sentences.

"I don't want to play jump rope today," Elizabeth said to Jessica. "I think the boys are going to play soccer."

"Not that again," Jessica said with a sigh. She walked out of the classroom with Lila Fowler.

Todd Wilkins and Jim Sturbridge were standing near Elizabeth's desk. "Do you want to watch us practice, Elizabeth?" Jim teased.

Elizabeth shook her head. "No. I want to play."

"But we have to practice for real," Todd said. "We're signing up for the soccer league.

3

We only have until a week from Saturday to practice."

"So am I," Elizabeth said. "The Sweet Valley Soccer League is open to boys *and* girls."

Todd and Jim looked at each other. "Really?" Jim asked.

Eva Simpson walked over to the group. "I'm trying out, too," she said.

Elizabeth smiled. "That's great."

"I learned to play in Jamaica," Eva said. She had moved to Sweet Valley from Jamaica, an island in the West Indies.

"Hey," Jim called out to the boys who were still in the classroom. "Elizabeth and Eva are going out for the soccer league."

Ken Matthews, Charlie Cashman, and Ricky Capaldo came over. "*They're* signing up for soccer?" Ken said.

"So?" Elizabeth said. She didn't under-

4

stand why the boys were acting so silly all of a sudden. "I play with you all the time at the park. What's the difference?"

Charlie pretended to kick a ball, and then he imitated a girl's voice. "Ow! I stubbed my toe! It hurts!"

All of the boys laughed. Elizabeth folded her arms and frowned. "What's so funny?" she demanded. "I can try out for the soccer league."

"Sure, you can *try out,*" Todd said. He looked at the other boys and grinned. "Anyone can show up. It's just that you won't make the first team. Most boys play better than girls."

Elizabeth stared at Todd. She couldn't believe he meant what he was saying. He lived near her, and they played softball and soccer together all the time. Todd was always glad

6

to have her on his team when they played in the park.

"That's not true and you know it, Todd Wilkins!" she said angrily. "I'm just as good as you are."

Instead of answering, the boys laughed and walked out of the classroom. Elizabeth looked at Eva.

"We'll show them," she said.

Eva nodded. "We can make the team any time we want to."

Elizabeth nodded, too. She wanted to make the team more than anything else in the world now.

CHAPTER 2

The Dance Recital

After school, Jessica and Elizabeth went to modern-dance class. They changed into their leotards and leg-warmers in the dressing room and then went into the studio. Jessica looked around quickly to see where Lila Fowler and Ellen Riteman were.

"Hi, Jessica," Lila called out. She and Ellen were practicing turns in front of the mirror.

"Is Elizabeth really trying out for soccer?" Ellen asked when Jessica walked up.

Jessica stretched her legs and frowned. "Yes."

"She's such a tomboy," Lila said.

"Playing soccer doesn't mean she's a tomboy," Jessica said quickly. Jessica didn't like anyone to criticize her sister. "She's good at soccer and she likes it," she said.

Lila smiled but didn't say anything. She was always a know-it-all about things.

"Attention, class!" the dance teacher, Ms. Garber, said. "I have an announcement to make."

Jessica ran over to sit on the floor next to Elizabeth.

"The advanced ballet students at Madame Andre's Dance Studio are having their annual recital next week," Ms. Garber said. "It would be a good chance for you girls to see how ballet is different from modern dance.

Some of you may want to start taking ballet lessons in the next few years."

Elizabeth and Jessica grinned at each other and clapped their hands silently. "That'll be fun!" Elizabeth whispered. "I can't wait."

"I know," Jessica said. "Ballet is so pretty and graceful."

Sandra Bacon held up her hand. "What day will it be, Ms. Garber?"

"Next Saturday afternoon," the teacher answered.

Elizabeth gulped. "That's the day of the soccer try out!" she whispered.

"Then I guess you can't sign up," Jessica said.

Elizabeth didn't answer. That wasn't what she had in mind.

"And now, class, let's get started on our warm-ups," Ms. Garber said.

11

While everyone stood up and began to stretch, Jessica looked over at Elizabeth.

"Don't you love ballet?" Jessica whispered when she did a graceful bend in Elizabeth's direction.

Elizabeth did a bend the other way. "Yes," she said.

"So that means you want to go to the recital?" Jessica went on.

"Yes," Elizabeth said sadly.

"Who needs dumb soccer anyway?" Jessica said. She thought that Elizabeth would forget about the soccer league now.

But Elizabeth shook her head. "I'm still going to try out," she explained. "I'm sad I'm going to miss the recital."

"You can't!" Jessica said. "We do everything together." Jessica felt it wouldn't be any fun if Elizabeth made the soccer team.

What would she do while her sister was off practicing and playing games?

Elizabeth seemed to read her sister's thoughts. "Why don't you try out for the soccer team, too?" she suggested. "We could both do it."

Jessica shook her head. "No. I want to go to the ballet recital. Besides, I don't like soccer."

"Oh." Elizabeth raised her arms over her head and twirled around.

"Are you still going to try out?" Lila interrupted from behind them.

Elizabeth looked over her shoulder. "Probably," she said.

"How can you even like soccer?" Lila asked in her snobby way. "It's so dirty and rough."

"But it's fun," Elizabeth answered.

Jessica looked at Lila and shook her head.

She wished her friend would be quiet, but Lila just ignored her.

"Soccer is a boy's sport," Lila went on.

"Lots of girls play soccer," Elizabeth pointed out. "And you know it."

"Well, I think going to a ballet recital is more interesting than soccer," Lila continued.

Jessica shook her head again and widened her eyes. She knew Elizabeth would disagree with whatever Lila said. Elizabeth often called Lila "Miss Bossy Fowler" behind her back.

"It's not better," Elizabeth said seriously. "They're both good."

Lila made a face.

Elizabeth looked at Jessica. "Nobody wants me to be on the soccer league," she said. "First Todd, then Lila, and even you.

Well, I'm going out for the soccer league no matter what anybody says," she continued firmly. "And I'm going to make the team. So there."

Jessica sighed. Now there was no way Elizabeth was going to change her mind.

CHAPTER 3

Practice, Practice, Practice

Over the weekend, Elizabeth invited Eva over so they could practice soccer kicks together. Eva had real soccer shoes with strong plastic cleats. "They used to belong to my cousin who lives in England now," she explained. "They play soccer all the time there."

"Those are neat," Elizabeth said, admiring the shoes. She was excited about the soccer tryouts. "Let's go into the backyard."

"Do you have your own soccer ball?" Eva asked.

Elizabeth nodded. "It's my brother's."

When they stepped outside, they saw Steven bouncing the soccer ball on his knee. "Hi," he greeted them. "Want me to help coach you?"

"Would you?" Elizabeth asked happily. Steven was two years older and had been in the soccer league for two years.

"No problem," he said. "I'll bet you're good, Eva."

Eva smiled shyly, "I'm OK, but I can always use some pointers."

"Then let's start," Steven said. "Practice passing the ball back and forth between you."

Elizabeth concentrated hard on kicking and stopping the soccer ball with her foot. At first, she and Eva stood just a few feet apart to pass the ball. Then Steven told them to move two steps farther apart each time. Soon, they were on opposite sides of the yard.

"Now try it while you're running," Steven said. "Keep your eye on the ball!"

Elizabeth couldn't stop smiling. It was so much fun! She tapped the ball lightly with her feet while she ran and then kicked it hard to Eva.

"Good one!" Steven yelled. "Do you want to try catching it, in case they ask you to be goalie?"

The smile on Elizabeth's face disappeared. "Well, um . . ."

"Sure," Eva said. "I like being goalie."

Steven kicked the ball in the air toward Eva, and she caught it against her stomach. Elizabeth bit her lip.

"Didn't that hurt?" she asked.

"Not really," Eva said.

Elizabeth looked away. She was nervous about trying to catch the soccer ball. Once

20

when she had tried it, the ball had hit her in the face and given her a bloody nose. Since then, she had avoided being the goalie. She knew it was silly, but she was afraid of getting hurt.

"Come on, Elizabeth," Steven said. "It's your turn."

Elizabeth felt very anxious. "I have to tie my shoelace," she said quickly.

"Let me try again," Eva said while Elizabeth sat down on the grass.

Elizabeth watched her brother help Eva. She wondered what would happen if she had to catch a soccer ball during the tryouts. She knew she had to do it, so she took a deep breath and stood up.

"OK, I'm ready," she said.

"Coming at you!" Steven said. He aimed a kick right at her.

21

Elizabeth closed her eyes. She couldn't help it. The ball bounced off her knees and rolled away.

"That would have been a score for the other team," Eva said. "Why don't you try it again?"

"Li-listen, I was thinking," Elizabeth stammered. "I'm not going to try out for goalie, so I don't think I need to practice this."

Steven shook his head. "They make you try all positions during practice. Come on."

Elizabeth knew she was acting like a baby. Usually, she wasn't afraid of any sport. She loved softball, gymnastics, running, and basketball. But every time she thought about being goalie, it scared her.

She still wanted to be on the soccer league, though. But how could she, if she couldn't catch the soccer ball?

CHAPTER 4

Lonely Jessica

Jessica was upstairs in the twins' bedroom. When she heard Eva say goodbye to Elizabeth, she ran to the window and looked into the backyard. Elizabeth was by herself, kicking the soccer ball forward, running to stop it, and kicking it backward. Jessica watched her sister for a moment.

Then she looked at the videotape from the public library that was sitting on her bed. It was a ballet performance of *Sleeping Beauty*.

"Liz!" she yelled out the window.

Elizabeth looked up.

"Do you want to watch *Sleeping Beauty* with me?" Jessica asked.

Elizabeth shaded her eyes with one hand. "Not now, Jess. I'm still practicing."

"But we have to return it to the library soon," Jessica said. "It's supposed to be really, really good."

"Maybe later," Elizabeth shouted.

Jessica frowned. She went downstairs to the den and put the tape into the video player. Music filled the room, as on the screen dancers in beautiful costumes came onstage. Jessica pushed the *pause* button and ran to the back door. "Liz, it's starting! I'll wait for you!" she called.

"Go ahead and watch it," Elizabeth answered. She bounced the soccer ball on her knee. It was leaving muddy marks all over her leg.

24

Jessica made a face. "You're getting all dirty," she said.

"That's because the ground is wet and I fell a few times," Elizabeth said happily. "Besides, if it rains during a game, I'll get covered in mud anyway."

"Yuck!" Jessica pretended to shiver. "That sounds icky!"

Elizabeth laughed. "I think it would be fun. I could pretend to be a pig in a pigpen."

The idea of rolling in the mud like a pig didn't sound good to Jessica. "Wouldn't you like to watch this ballet movie instead?" she begged. "The dancers have beautiful costumes on."

"It sounds nice," Elizabeth said. She bounced the soccer ball on the ground and caught it. "Maybe you could do some kicks with me, and then we could watch it."

Jessica fiddled with the doorknob. "But I don't have my play clothes on," she said.

"You could put them on," Elizabeth pointed out.

"I think they're in the laundry basket," Jessica said.

Elizabeth shrugged. "You could borrow some of mine."

"Liz, I don't *want* to play soccer," Jessica finally said. "I don't want to get all muddy and grass-stained even in play clothes. *"I just don't like soccer!"*

Elizabeth looked at Jessica, and Jessica looked back at Elizabeth. This was the first time they wanted to do different things.

"I have to keep practicing," Elizabeth said quietly. She looked at the ground. "If I don't practice, I won't be good enough to make the team."

"Are you sure you don't want to come in and watch the ballet movie?" Jessica pleaded one last time. "Then you'll change your mind and come to the recital with me next Saturday."

Elizabeth shook her head. "I'm sorry, Jess. I'm going to play soccer."

With a loud sigh, Jessica turned around and went back into the house. It looked like ballet was one thing she would have to do without her twin.

CHAPTER 5

Boys Against Girls

Elizabeth placed her tray on the cafeteria table and sat in the seat next to Jessica. "What kind of sandwich did Mom make for us today?" she asked.

"Tuna squish," Jessica answered with a smile. It was her way of saying tuna fish.

"Our favorite," Elizabeth said. She looked around the lunchroom and saw Eva coming out of the milk line. "Sit here!" she said, waving her hand.

Eva hurried over. "Ouch," she said as she

sat down. "I've got a bruise on my leg from the soccer ball that hit me on Saturday."

"Sorry," Elizabeth said. "I didn't mean to kick the ball so hard."

"It's OK. You get hit a lot when you play in games," Eva said in a matter-of-fact way.

"I sure hope you aren't a crybaby," Ken Matthews said from three seats down.

"Yeah," Todd joined in. "We're not going to be careful just because you're playing with us."

Elizabeth put her sandwich down and looked at Todd. "You don't have to be. We're just as good as you are."

"I think we're even better," Eva whispered in Elizabeth's ear.

"So do I," Elizabeth answered. She was still worried about being goalie, but she had almost a week to practice. Elizabeth felt angry that the boys kept making jokes about girls trying out. She knew she and Eva were better than many of the boys. Why did they have to tease so much?

"Listen," Charlie said in a know-it-all way. "They always let girls sign up. But you're never going to make the team. You're a bunch of crybabies."

The boys started laughing, but Jessica stood up and banged her fist on the table. "We are not!" she shouted.

Elizabeth was surprised. So was everyone else.

"Elizabeth is my sister and she never cries if she gets hurt. Unless it's really, *really* bad," Jessica said firmly.

"Oh, sure," Jim Sturbridge said.

Lila spoke up. "I'll bet Elizabeth and Eva are better than all of you put together."

"No way!" Ken said loudly.

"Just you wait and see," Ellen chimed in.

Elizabeth was glad her girl-friends were sticking up for her, but she was sorry that everyone was fighting. She and Eva had really stirred up trouble, and she couldn't figure out why. Usually everyone in class got along. *What has happened?* she wondered.

Now everyone at the lunch table was in the argument. The girls were shouting at the boys, and the boys were shouting at the girls.

"What's all this commotion?" Mrs. Otis broke in.

Mr. Butler, the gym teacher, followed. "What's going on?"

"The boys say they're better than we are!" Jessica explained.

"Why do they say that?" Mrs. Otis asked.

All the boys looked down at their lunches and were silent.

"It's because Eva and I are trying out for the soccer league," Elizabeth said. "They say we won't make the team that gets to play all the time."

Mrs. Otis sighed. "Oh, really?" she said. "I'm sure you'll make the team. But sometimes when girls are teased, they don't always do as well."

"That's right," Mr. Butler said. "Girls are able to play soccer very well, as long as they don't feel embarrassed about playing. In fact, at your age, many girls are better players than boys."

Everyone at the table was silent. Elizabeth glanced at Eva and smiled.

"Now I don't want to hear any more of this

boys-better-than-girls nonsense," Mrs. Otis said as she walked away with Mr. Butler.

As soon as she was gone, Jessica laughed. "See?" she said. "Mrs. Otis and Mr. Butler are on our side."

"Who cares?" Charlie grumbled.

Elizabeth rolled her eyes. The boys would never believe she and Eva were good enough unless they made the team.

There was no way Elizabeth was going to miss the tryouts now—even if she did have to be goalie. She would show them!

CHAPTER 6

A Little Help

On Wednesday afternoon, Jessica and Elizabeth walked home from the bus stop together. Elizabeth was unusually quiet.

"What's wrong?" Jessica asked.

Elizabeth shrugged. "I don't know," she said, kicking a pebble. "I guess I'm just mad that Todd keeps making fun of me because of the soccer tryouts."

"I'll bet he's just afraid you'll be better than he is," Jessica said confidently.

Elizabeth looked at her and smiled. "Do you really think so?"

"Sure," Jessica said.

"I don't know," Elizabeth said. She wasn't smiling anymore. "Remember when I got a bloody nose playing soccer last year? Well, I'm still afraid to catch the ball."

Jessica made a face. "I remember," she said. "It was horrible."

"What if it happens again?" Elizabeth's voice quivered. "That's what I keep getting scared of."

Jessica didn't know what to say. It was unusual for Elizabeth to sound so nervous. "You're still going to go to the tryouts, right?" she asked.

"Well . . . I guess so." Elizabeth kicked another pebble. "But what if I have to be goalie? Then the boys will think they were right. And maybe they are. Maybe I am a cry baby."

"That's not true!" Jessica said quickly. "You always play well. So you have to try out. I'll even help you practice if you want!"

"You will?" Elizabeth asked. They stopped at their front door and looked at each other. Elizabeth's worried expression changed to a big smile. "You might get dirty, you know."

"That's OK," Jessica decided. "I can always take a bath.

They both laughed and went inside. Maybe they didn't always like the same things, but they were still the very best friends.

Elizabeth went to Eva's house after school on Friday. Eva's father had once been a soccer coach, and he had promised to help them get ready for the tryouts. Elizabeth was excited about visiting the Simpsons, because the family was so friendly and interesting.

Mrs. Simpson was a flute player in the local orchestra. She was practicing in an upstairs room when Elizabeth and Eva walked into the house.

"Hello, Mother!" Eva called out.

The flute playing stopped. "Do I hear the World Cup soccer champions?" came a cheerful voice.

The girls both laughed. "Hello, Mrs. Simpson!" Elizabeth shouted.

Eva's mother came downstairs and gave them both a kiss. "I'll get you something light to eat before you go out to practice," she said, leading the way to the kitchen. "That way you'll have a bit more energy."

"Let me show you these pictures," Eva said

while they both had milk and cookies. She took a photograph album from a shelf and opened it to a page in the middle. "See? Here I am playing soccer on my school team in Jamaica," she said.

Elizabeth smiled. Usually, Eva was quiet and shy at school. But in her own home, she was outgoing.

"Were you the goalie?" Elizabeth asked. She was impressed that Eva could play the position she was afraid to play.

"Yes. It was fun," Eva said with a big grin. "We should practice that this afternoon."

"What's this? What's this?" Mr. Simpson came into the house from the backyard and put his arm around Eva's shoulders. "Out on the field, you lazy things!" he said.

Laughing, Eva and Elizabeth ran out the door to the backyard. Elizabeth was sure she

would learn how to catch the soccer ball today.

She had to. The soccer tryout was only one
day away.

CHAPTER 7

The Big Day

Everyone was getting ready to leave the house on Saturday afternoon. Mr. Wakefield was taking Jessica to the ballet recital, and Mrs. Wakefield was going with Elizabeth to the soccer tryouts.

"Are you nervous?" Jessica said to her sister.

Elizabeth's cheeks were pink. "A little bit," she admitted. "I hope you have fun at the recital."

"Thanks," Jessica said. She looked slightly nervous, too. "Here comes Dad."

"And here comes Mom," Elizabeth said at the same time.

"Wait up!" Steven yelled. He ran down the stairs. "I'm coming with you, Elizabeth," he said.

Elizabeth looked at her brother and smiled. Usually, he didn't want to do anything with his little sisters, but today was special. She knew he wanted to cheer her on at the tryouts. She gave him a big hug.

Jessica waved and climbed into their father's car and waved goodbye. "Good luck! I hope you make the team!" she called.

By the time Elizabeth arrived at the high school athletic field, her stomach was in a knot. She retied the laces on her sneakers.

"You'll do fine, honey," Mrs. Wakefield said. Steven gave her a thumbs-up sign.

Elizabeth looked around the field. There

were about ten other girls trying out. The rest were boys.

"Isn't this exciting?" Eva asked when she saw Elizabeth.

"I think so," Elizabeth said. She smiled at Mr. Simpson. "I'm going to remember everything you taught us yesterday," she said.

Mr. Simpson ruffled her hair. "That's my girl. The most important thing is to keep your eye on the ball. You should always know where it is."

Elizabeth and Eva both nodded. A man with a clipboard began calling for attention.

"Line up!" the coach yelled. "My name is Jim Wilson. I want everyone to warm up by running two times around the field."

Everyone groaned, but Elizabeth was ready for anything. "I can run pretty fast," she whispered to Eva.

"Me, too," Eva whispered back.

It wasn't a race, but Elizabeth and Eva ran as fast as they could. Elizabeth was excited to see that they were both faster than a lot of the boys.

"Look out!" she called as she raced past Todd and Ken.

The two of them looked surprised. "Hey!" Todd shouted. "You'll never be able to finish."

Elizabeth ignored him. She would show him that girls could be just as good at sports as boys.

"Come on," she said to Eva, who was running at her side. As they finished their second lap, Elizabeth didn't feel tired at all. She felt like she could run all afternoon!

When everyone was finished, Coach Wilson dragged a giant bag of soccer balls

onto the field and asked everyone to line up.

"One at a time, I want you to run toward me," the coach explained. "I'll roll a soccer ball in your direction and I want you to kick it to the left side of the field. The next person will kick it to the right side of the field. Got it?" he shouted.

"Got it!" everyone yelled back.

Elizabeth hopped from one foot to the other. She couldn't wait for her turn. She knew she would be able to kick the ball far.

"Are you starting to get worried, Wakefield?" Charlie Cashman asked.

Elizabeth turned around and stuck her tongue out at Charlie. Then she looked at Eva and grinned. She was too excited to worry about the boys teasing her anymore.

The line was moving ahead as the kids ran up for their turn. Soccer balls were zooming all over the field, and the coach's helpers were picking them up. Soon, there were only two people ahead of Elizabeth: Todd and another boy.

"Let's go! Let's go!" the coach yelled as he rolled the ball toward Todd.

Todd ran up and kicked the ball so hard it went *boof* and sailed way up into the air. He kept running and raised his hands over his head in a victory sign.

"I can do even better," Elizabeth whispered to herself.

The next second, it was her turn. She ran toward the coach, keeping her eyes on the soccer ball in his hands. When he rolled it toward her, she sped up, aimed her foot, and slammed the ball.

"*Boof!*" The ball shot along the ground like a bullet. The assistant who was supposed to catch it jumped out of the way.

"Way to go, Elizabeth!" Eva screamed.

Elizabeth breathed a sigh of relief. So far, so good.

CHAPTER 8

At the Recital

Jessica thought the ballet recital was wonderful. The boy dancers jumped high and the ballerinas spun across the stage. It was like a fairy tale.

But even though Jessica was watching every step, she was thinking about Elizabeth, too. She knew how important the soccer league was to her sister. As soon as the recital was over, she grabbed her father's hand.

"Can we go to the high school field?" she

asked eagerly. "Maybe the tryouts aren't over yet."

"Don't you want to meet some of the dancers?" Mr. Wakefield said.

Jessica shook her head. "I'd rather go watch Elizabeth."

"OK," Mr. Wakefield agreed. "If we hurry, we can catch the last part of the tryouts."

"Good!" Jessica said, jumping up and down. "Let's go!"

In just a few minutes, they reached Sweet Valley High School. Jessica could see lots of cars in the parking area, which meant the tryouts were still going on.

"Hurry, Dad!" she said as they got out of the car. She ran to the field and looked over the crowd until she saw her mother and Steven. "Did we miss a lot?"

"They're starting a practice game," Steven told her. "Elizabeth is center forward!"

It only took Jessica two seconds to spot her sister out on the field. Elizabeth was running after a boy who had control of the soccer ball. Elizabeth cut in front of him and stole the ball away with a short kick.

"YEA!" Jessica screamed. "GO, LIZ!"

Elizabeth started running and dribbling the ball toward the goal. She dodged around an opponent and kicked the ball into the net.

"YEA!" Jessica screamed even louder and jumped up and down. "Liz scored, Mom!"

"I know!" Mrs. Wakefield laughed and clapped her hands.

Mr. Wakefield put two fingers in his mouth and let out a piercing whistle. The tryouts were so exciting that Jessica almost wished she were out on the field, too!

"Where's Eva?" Jessica asked.

Steven pointed to the opposite end of the field. Eva was guarding the goal.

"Do you think someone's going to kick a ball at her?" she asked.

Her brother shrugged. "Maybe. Watch."

One player was running with the ball and the coach was running up and down the sidelines to see how each player did. Todd sneaked the ball away from the player and headed down toward Eva.

"Look out!" Jessica yelled. "Here comes Todd!"

Eva had a very serious expression on her face. She stood with her feet wide apart and her hands out. She looked ready for anything!

Suddenly, Todd twisted around and kicked the ball in a slanting line toward the net. Eva dived headfirst for the ball and grabbed it in midair!

"WAY TO GO!" Mr. Simpson jumped up and down and waved his arms. "FIRST RATE, EVA! GOOD SHOW!"

Jessica cheered and clapped her hands. It looked like Eva would make the team for sure.

"Eva should be the goalie," Mr. Wakefield said. "She's fearless."

"You'd never know it from looking at her," Mrs. Wakefield said with a laugh. "She's usually so sweet. But on the soccer field, she's tough!"

Jessica hoped people would say the same thing about Elizabeth. Maybe Lila would say that she was a tomboy, but Jessica didn't care. She wanted everyone to notice how good her sister was.

"GO, LIZ!" she yelled.

Elizabeth ran past where her family was standing. Jessica was able to catch her eye and wave. Elizabeth waved back, then chased after the soccer ball again.

"I hope she makes the team," Jessica wished softly. "Please, please, please let her make the team."

There was only one thing that could get in the way now. What if the coach put Elizabeth in the goal? Jessica crossed her fingers and wished that that wouldn't happen.

Elizabeth's side scored two more goals, and Eva again stopped the other team from making a goal of their own. The coach blew his whistle.

"OK!" he shouted. "SAME TEAMS, DIF-
FERENT POSITIONS!"

He began pointing to people and assigning
them new positions to play. Finally, he
looked right at Elizabeth.

Jessica held her breath.

"Goalie!" he said.

The expression on Elizabeth's face made
Jessica feel awful.

Mr. Wakefield cupped his hands and
shouted, "YOU CAN DO IT, LIZ!"

Elizabeth looked over at her family and
tried to smile. But Jessica knew exactly how
she felt inside. She was terrified!

CHAPTER 9

Goalie

Elizabeth took a deep breath. Maybe she would be lucky, and no one would kick the ball toward the goal.

But she knew that was too much to hope for.

"What's wrong, Elizabeth?" Todd asked her. "You look like you want to run away."

"I do not!" Elizabeth yelled back. She glared at him. "You're being a big pain in the neck, Todd Wilkins. Stop making fun of me!"

Todd pretended to be frightened. Then he looked over at Jim and laughed.

"Say you're sorry," Elizabeth went on angrily. "Or I'll never talk to you again."

"I will if you make the team," Todd answered. Then the coach blew his whistle again, and Todd waved. "Time to go to your goal, Elizabeth."

Elizabeth felt sad inside. She never realized that Todd could hurt her feelings so much. She walked slowly down the field.

"Good luck," Eva said as they traded places.

"Thanks," Elizabeth answered. "I think I need it."

Elizabeth stood out in front of the net and tried to feel confident. Maybe it wouldn't matter if she didn't catch the ball, she thought. The coach already knew she was good at running, dribbling, passing, kicking, and scoring.

But then she decided that if she was good at all those things, she could be a good goalie, too. She wanted someone to kick the ball at her! She wanted to show everyone she could catch it. She wanted to prove she wasn't afraid.

Eva wasn't afraid, and Elizabeth didn't want to be, either.

She looked over at the sidelines. Her family waved, and so did Eva's father. "Keep your eyes on the ball," Elizabeth said to herself. "Keep your eyes on the ball."

The game started. Elizabeth watched the ball carefully. Whenever it started to come closer to her end, she got ready.

But for a long time, no one kicked it toward her at all. Suddenly, Todd stole the ball away from Eva, and began kicking it down the field toward Elizabeth. He kicked it across to Jim, and they passed it back and forth.

They were getting closer and closer. Eva was chasing after Todd. She was trying to cut in front of him and kick the ball away. But Todd kept getting away from her.

"Get it, Eva!" Elizabeth yelled.

Elizabeth's palms were sweating. She knew that if Eva didn't get the ball, *she* would have to stop it.

Eva stole the ball away from Todd, but then Todd ran in front of her and got the ball back in his control. He spun around and aimed for the goal.

Without even thinking, Elizabeth jumped to catch it. She kept her eyes wide open and held her arms out. The ball landed right in her hands.

Elizabeth wrapped her arms around the ball and held it tight. "Oof!" she gasped.

Todd stopped and looked at her. "You caught it!" he said in surprise.

"Throw the ball back into play!" Coach Wilson yelled.

Elizabeth tossed the ball out to Eva, who stopped it with her knee. Then she dribbled to the opposite end of the field, far away from Elizabeth.

"I did it!" Elizabeth said out loud to herself. She grinned from ear to ear.

The coach looked over at her to give her a thumbs-up sign. Elizabeth had never felt prouder in her life.

CHAPTER 10

Victory!

By the time the tryouts were over, Jessica had screamed herself into a sore throat. "I know she'll make the team," she said hoarsely to her parents.

"I'm sure she will," Mr. Wakefield said with a smile. "I'm so proud of her."

The soccer players were all sitting on the grass around the coach. They looked dirty, tired, and very, very excited.

"I'm going to sit with Liz," Jessica announced. She ran over and sat on the grass next to her twin. "Hi."

Elizabeth was breathing hard. "Hi," she said with a big smile. There was a dirty smudge on her cheek, and her hands and knees were grass-stained. She looked very happy.

"Now listen up, everyone," the coach said. "I'm going to pick some of you to be the first string. Sometimes it's called the starting lineup. That means you'll be the ones to start each game, and the rest of you will go in as substitutes when you're needed."

Everyone was whispering and wondering who would make the team. Jessica crossed her fingers.

"Let me have Capaldo!" The coach read from his clipboard. "Matthews! Simpson! Finn!"

Each time a name was called, the person jumped up and ran to stand beside the coach.

Elizabeth was thrilled that Eva made it. She stared at the coach with a hopeful expression. He read off several more names.

Then he read off "Wilkins!" and Todd stood up.

"Too bad, Elizabeth," he whispered.

"He's not finished reading yet!" Elizabeth said.

"Wakefield!"

"Hooray!" Elizabeth cheered as she jumped up. "I did it!"

Elizabeth and Eva hugged each other.

"Now what do you say, Todd?" Elizabeth asked.

Todd looked embarrassed. He reached over and punched Elizabeth in the shoulder. "You played a good game," he muttered.

When the coach was finished reading the names of the first string players, he had

more announcements. "Practice will be Mondays and Wednesdays after school," he said. "Our first game is in three weeks."

Jessica looked at Elizabeth. "I knew you could do it," she told her sister.

"Don't you wish you were on the team, too?" Elizabeth said excitedly. "I wish you were."

"Well . . ." Jessica began. "Not really. But I'm coming to every game you play."

Mr. and Mrs. Wakefield and Steven came over, and Elizabeth got hugs and kisses from everyone.

"It's time to celebrate," Mr. Wakefield announced. "We're going out to Bingo Burgers for dinner."

Elizabeth and Jessica both cheered. It was the perfect way to start the soccer season!

Jessica finished her dinner before everyone else. She stood up from the table and tapped her mother's arm.

"Can I get the recital program from the car, Mom?" she asked. "I want to show it to Liz."

Mrs. Wakefield nodded. "Sure. Hurry back, though."

"I will." Jessica ran out of the Bingo Burgers restaurant and headed to the parking lot.

A familiar car was just pulling in. Mr. and Mrs. DeVito got out with their new baby, Jenny. The DeVitos were the Wakefields' neighbors.

"Hi!" Jessica called.

Mrs. DeVito gave her a big smile. "Well, hello, Elizabeth."

"Hi, Jessica," Mr. DeVito said at the same

time. Mr. and Mrs. DeVito looked at each other and laughed.

Jessica grinned. Many people mistook her for Elizabeth. It happened all the time.

"Well, which twin are you?" Mrs. DeVito asked.

"I'm Elizabeth," Jessica answered. Her eyes sparkled mischievously.

"You were right, Sue," Mr. DeVito said to his wife. "Well, Elizabeth, I guess we're having dinner at the same place. We'll see you inside."

Jessica decided she would tell them who she really was when they all got inside. But it was fun to pretend to be Elizabeth.

Will Jessica get in trouble pretending to be Elizabeth? Find out in Sweet Valley Kids #16, JESSICA THE TV STAR.